SUPERHERO JASEY

EMY JONES

Illustrated by Dennis Davide

To order additional copies of this book, contact:
Xlibris
1-888-795-4274
www.Xlibris.com
Orders@Xlibris.com

ISBN: Softcover   978-1-7960-6208-3
         Hardcover   978-1-7960-6209-0
         EBook   978-1-7960-6207-6

Print information available on the last page

Rev. date: 09/26/2019

NOTE TO READER

At the end of this book, you will be able to surprise your little listener with a superpower of your own. This can change with each reading and could include hugging, kissing, tickling, chasing, laughing, juggling, or singing a favorite song. Your listener will be waiting with anticipation to see which superpower you show him or her this time.

Once upon a time, there was a brave and handsome superhero named Dad. What was his superpower? You'll soon find out.

Far, far away, there lived a dazzling and daring superhero named Mom. Don't worry. You'll soon learn what her superpower is too.

One magical day, they met while they were saving lives in the sky. And yep! You guessed it. They fell in love! Mom and Dad were happy.

But the best was yet to come. They still hadn't asked each other the biggest question. What question?

"What is your superpower?"

"What is *your* superpower?"

It was amazing. They found out that they had the same superpowers! Wow, can you believe it?

They were joyful. Things really could not be better. Or could they?

Dad and Mom were about to be even happier.

You see, they loved each other so much that they had a beautiful baby. Her name was Jasey.

Now life got really fun.

Everyone loved that baby Jasey so much.

One exciting day, they found out ... what?

Guess what? Jasey would be a superhero too.

8

Dad and Mom had a lot of work to do. What kind of superpowers would Jasey have?

They wanted Jasey to be the best superhero ever, so Mom and Dad taught her some really great superpowers.

They taught her to be careful but brave.

Jasey watched Mom and Dad and learned how to take care of her little brother, James.

They helped her to become strong.

They taught her that sometimes it's okay to be sad.

But Jasey also learned how much fun it is to be happy.

They showed her that reading is one of the biggest superpowers ever.

And that learning is so much fun.

Jasey also learned that hugs are awesome.

When Jasey learned how to use all these superpowers, she was ready.

So go put on your cape, Superhero Jasey. It's time to save the world!

Dad and Mom were proud of Jasey because she was ready to use her

superpowers to make the world a better place.

Jasey's Guide to Superpowers

BE STRONG.

BE KIND.

READ.

LOVE.

HAVE FUN.

LEARN.

BE BRAVE.

Each day, Jasey tried to use at least one of her superpowers.

Now, are you ready to find out what Daddy and Mommy's superpowers are? Are you sure? I wonder which one they'll show you today. Okay, if you're really ready, turn the page. Wait for it.

Printed in the United States
By Bookmasters